Row, Row, Row Your Boat

Jane Cabrera

Holiday House / New York

Row, row, row your boat
Gently down the stream.
Merrily, merrily, merrily, merrily,
Life is but a dream.

Row, row, row your boat
Slowly down the creek.
If you see the swimming mice,
Don't forget to squeak.
EEEEK!

Row, row, row your boat.
Splish! and Splash! and Splatter!
If you see the monkeys swing,
Don't forget to chatter.
OO, OO, AH, AH!

Row, row, row your boat
Past the old tree stump.
If you see the elephant,
Don't forget to trump!
BARAAAAH!

Row, row, row your boat
Through the narrow gap.
If you see a crocodile,
Don't forget to snap!
SNAP! SNAP!

Row, row, row your boat
Closer to the shore.
If you see a lion smile,
Don't forget to roar.
ROARRR!

Row, row, row your boat.
Watch the tiger prowl.
If you see his mighty pounce,
Don't forget to GROWL.
GRRRR!

Row, row, row your boat
Beneath the sky so blue.
If you see the singing doves,
Don't forget to coo.
COO!

Row, row, row your boat
Now it's getting dark.
If you see mommy dog,
Don't forget to bark.
WOOF!

Row, row, row your boat
Gently down the stream.
Wearily, wearily, wearily, wearily . . .

. . . snuggle up and dream.

Dedicated to all our planet's
disappearing forests
www.rainforestfoundation.org

Text and illustrations copyright © 2014 by Jane Cabrera
Musical arrangement of "Row, Row, Row Your Boat" copyright © 2014 by Holiday House
All Rights Reserved
Holiday House is registered in the U.S. Patent and Trademark Office.
Printed and Bound in November 2013
at Tien Wah Press, Johor Bahru, Johor, Malaysia.
The art was painted in acrylic paint, the same size as the book. The palettes were
old china plates. The artist started by tracing rough pencil drawings on paper
taped onto a window. The artist painted the black line, added the color,
and finished with a little more black line. The artist sometimes mixed
the color on the actual artwork rather than on the palette.
www.holidayhouse.com
First Edition
1 3 5 7 9 10 8 6 4 2

Library of Congress Cataloging-in-Publication Data
Cabrera, Jane, author, illustrator.
Row, row, row your boat / by Jane Cabrera. — First edition.
pages cm
Summary: In this expansion of a familiar song, the occupants of a rowboat
enjoy seeing and making the sounds of different jungle animals.
ISBN 978-0-8234-3050-5 (hardcover)
1. Children's songs, English—United States—Texts. [1. Jungle animals—Songs and music.
2. Animal sounds—Songs and music. 3. Boats and boating—Songs and music.
4. Songs.] I. Title.
PZ8.3.C122Row 2014
782.42083—dc23
[E]
2013027068

Row, Row, Row Your Boat

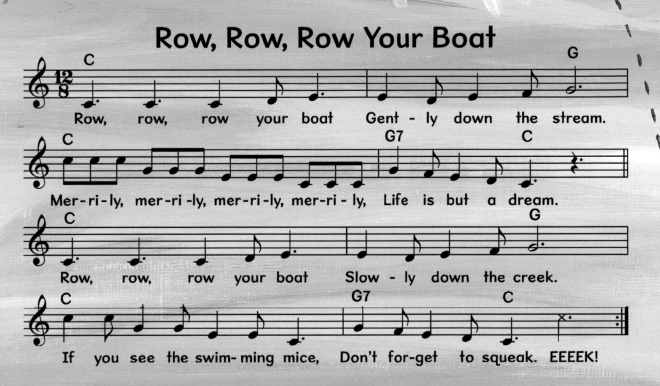

Row, row, row your boat Gent-ly down the stream.

Mer-ri-ly, mer-ri-ly, mer-ri-ly, mer-ri-ly, Life is but a dream.

Row, row, row your boat Slow-ly down the creek.

If you see the swim-ming mice, Don't for-get to squeak. EEEEK!

Row, row, row your boat.
Splish! and Splash! and Splatter!
If you see the monkeys swing,
Don't forget to chatter.
OO, OO, AH, AH!

Row, row, row your boat
Past the old tree stump.
If you see the elephant,
Don't forget to trump!
BARAAAAH!

Row, row, row your boat
Through the narrow gap.
If you see a crocodile,
Don't forget to snap!
SNAP! SNAP!

Row, row, row your boat
Closer to the shore.
If you see a lion smile,
Don't forget to roar.
ROARRR!

Row, row, row your boat.
Watch the tiger prowl.
If you see his mighty pounce,
Don't forget to GROWL.
GRRRR!

Row, row, row your boat
Beneath the sky so blue.
If you see the singing doves,
Don't forget to coo.
COO!

Row, row, row your boat
Now it's getting dark.
If you see mommy dog,
Don't forget to bark.
WOOF!

Row, row, row your boat
Gently down the stream.
Wearily, wearily, wearily, wearily...
...snuggle up and dream.